To my parents, George and Nadine O'Malley
&
My family, Gayle, Brianne and Collin

"Thanks for letting me chase my own rainbows"

SPECIAL THANKS TO

George O'malley Jr. for the illustration of the Yeti
Lynn LaGrange who was a great inspiration and mentor for this book
Kelly Wilcox for consulting on the production, Linda LaGrange for editing, and
Randy Troute for the digital cover art

The Secret of the Mountains

By

Brian O'Malley

Midge,
In your heart...
May you always want to
climb the highest
mountain!

Brian O'Malley

Illustrations by
Timothy Arp

Production and Design
Randy Troute

The Spirit of Adventure, Ltd.

Denver, Colorado

Introduction

n a far away land on the other side of the world lies the village of Namche Bazaar. It is tucked away in the Kingdom of Nepal, home of the mightiest mountain ranges on earth, the Himalaya.

High in the Himalaya is a region called the Khumbu, home of a tribe of people called Sherpas. The Sherpas help mountain climbers from all over the world by carrying heavy loads for long distances, often in their bare feet. They are a happy and proud people who survive their harsh mountain environment with a smile.

This is where Lopsong and Namka were born. Lopsong is a yak and Namka is a Sherpa boy. A yak is a high altitude animal that is used by the Sherpas to carry equipment and supplies to villages in their mountain homeland.

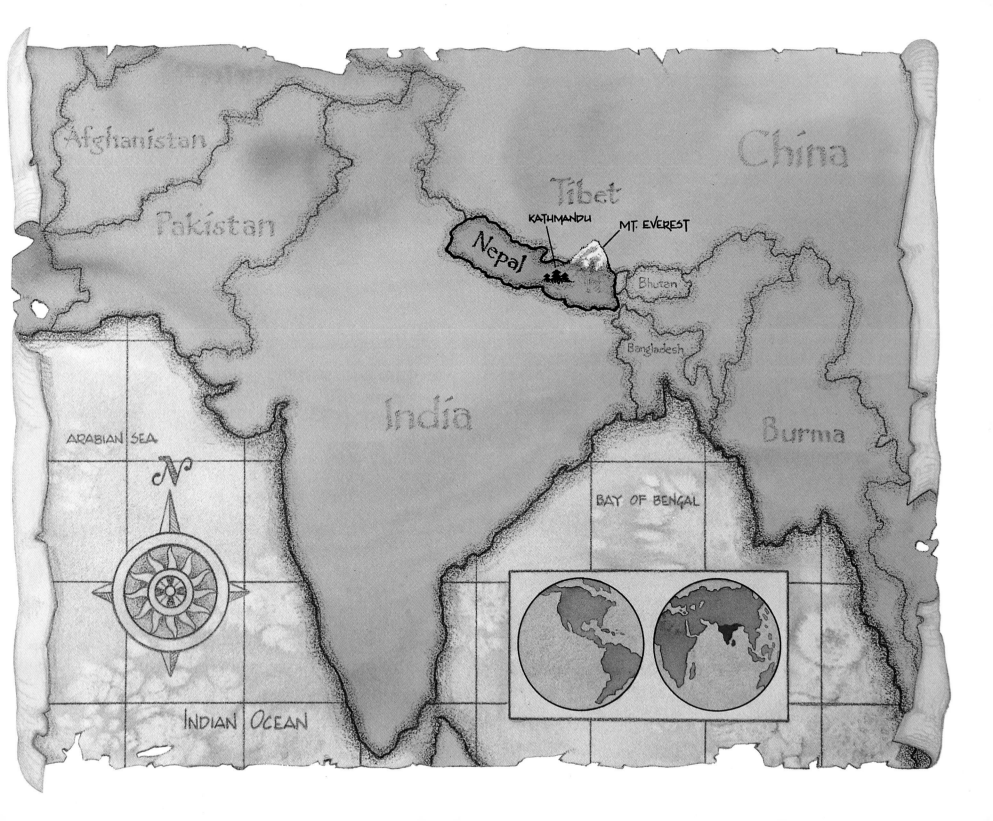

Namka snuggled close to the fire on this cold night listening to Grandpa Norkay tell stories about the mountains.

"Namka, the mountains are majestic, and they can teach us many lessons, but you must respect their power. Sometimes it snows so much that the steep slopes cannot hold all that snow, and it begins to slide.

Tons of heavy snow thunder downward taking everything in its path; it's called an avalanche. The roar of an avalanche can be heard far away.

Many of our people have lost their lives because of the avalanches," said Grandpa.

Namka's eyes were big as he imagined what an avalanche might look and sound like.

Grandpa continued, "As you know, Namka, it's important to practice your hiking and climbing so you are strong when you go into the mountains," said Grandpa.

"Oh, I will Grandpa. My yak, Lopsong, and I go every day to the river for water, and we carry as much as we can," boasted Namka. "Please, Grandpa, tell me about the Yeti," asked Namka.

"Well, Yeti means magical one, and I don't know of anyone who has actually seen a Yeti. The old stories say the Yeti is like a hairy monster that looks like a giant man with eyes that glow in the dark. He lives in the high snowy mountains. If you listen carefully when you're in the mountains, you can sometimes hear the eerie high-pitched whistle of the Yeti far off in the distance," Grandpa paused and whispered. "Sometimes people call him the Abominable Snowman."

One day when Lopsong was grazing in the field and dreaming about going on a mountain adventure, he heard the cheerful voice of his friend Namka. As Namka ran down the hill from school, he called out, "Lopsong, it's time to get water!"

There was no running water in Namka's home. Every day Namka and his yak would hike down to the river, then up the steep hills to bring the water home. Lopsong and Namka always had fun when they were together. Namka, being a Sherpa boy, carried his water with a tumpline, which was a strap that went under the water bucket and over his forehead. All Sherpas carry loads this way. Lopsong carried his load on his back like all yaks. It was hard work, but fun. They filled their buckets with water, and on their way back they pretended to be on a great adventure. Each day as they carried water up the steep hills, Namka and Lopsong grew stronger.

"Let's imagine we are on an adventure to Mount Everest!" bubbled Namka. They had never actually seen the mountain. Mount Everest is the tallest mountain in the world, and was located beyond the big hill near Lopsong and Namka's home. They'd always dreamed about going there.

Just then Namka and Lopsong heard a loud rumbling sound. It grew louder. They could feel the earth shake. "Is that an avalanche?" asked Namka, his voice trembling. "Oh, I'm sure it is, Lopsong, nothing else could be that powerful!" Namka held tightly onto Lopsong. Soon the sound began to fade.

One early morning, they set out on their own adventure to climb the big hill near their home. "I can't wait to get to the top," Namka said excitedly. Lopsong wagged his tail and shook his head in agreement. They climbed hard and the hill seemed to be getting bigger and bigger. As they climbed, they began feeling weaker and weaker. "Come on Lopsong. We are almost to the top," Namka encouraged his friend.

As they got higher, the air became thinner. Namka and Lopsong breathed harder. They took a few steps and then a deep breath. They were so tired that they couldn't talk. Lopsong was exhausted and fell to his knees. Namka stopped just short of the summit, and looked back at Lopsong, then back at the summit. They were so close. Not too much farther and they would be there. Namka had never seen such sadness in his friend's eyes before. He knew Lopsong couldn't go on, and Namka couldn't go to the top without him. They turned around, and after a short rest, they started carefully back down, both stumbling with fatigue.

oon it was dark. "It's not safe to hike in the darkness,"
Namka said, as he yawned. "We are so tired, we might get lost or
hurt. Let's rest here until the morning light. I've come prepared
with equipment to stay the night," remembering the lessons Grandpa
Norkay had taught him.

With a swish of Lopsong's tail, Namka knew his friend agreed they should
stop. They had never stayed alone before in the mountains at night.

"Do you think we'll see the Yeti tonight?" wondered Namka with his eyes
wide open. Once again Namka thought of the stories his grandpa had told
him. "Maybe he's watching us right now. It feels like he is,"
Namka said trying to keep his courage up.

No Yeti came. The next day they finally made it back home. Namka's mother and father were happy they were back safely. Namka and Lopsong were tired from their climbing, and also disappointed they hadn't made it to the top. "We learned a lot," Namka said. "It was a grand adventure, and we'll try for the summit another day."

O n their next try, they did get to the top. The view was awesome! It was more spectacular than they had imagined. They could see more mountains than they could count. "We did it!," Namka yelled to the wind. Lopsong pranced around with excitement. They both knew they were forever changed by what they had seen.

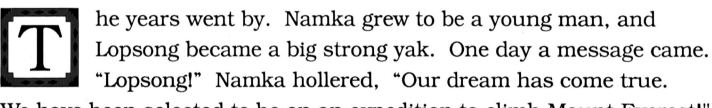

T he years went by. Namka grew to be a young man, and Lopsong became a big strong yak. One day a message came. "Lopsong!" Namka hollered, "Our dream has come true. We have been selected to be on an expedition to climb Mount Everest!"

That spring they joined the expedition. Their journey took them through many new and exciting villages and finally to the great Khumbu Glacier. It was a dangerous place, with big shifting slabs of ice. There were deep, dark cracks in the ice called crevasses.

N amka and Lopsong were proud to be a part of this expedition team. The team members had trained hard, and would need to work together to climb the giant mountain. It was cold, and the climbing was very difficult. For days the team worked it's way up the huge mountain of snow and ice.

After a long day of climbing, Namka turned to Lopsong and said excitedly, "Just think, soon we will be standing... on the top of the world!"

Suddenly they heard a terrifying sound! "An avalanche!" cried Namka, "Stay close, Lopsong!" The crushing wave of snow raged down the mountain with the sound of an explosion! Soon the deadly river of snow settled, and the avalanche was over. "Whew, we're okay," sighed Namka.

Just then, Namka saw that one of the climbers had been crushed by the avalanche. Lopsong and Namka swiftly uncovered the buried climber. He was badly hurt. Very carefully Namka helped put the injured climber on Lopsong's back.

As fast as they could, they carried him down to the base camp. He would need to be taken quickly to the small hospital in the village of Pheriche down in the valley.

When they reached the base camp Namka saw that a storm was coming. Everyone knew it would be risky to go across the glacier in the snowstorm. "Namka, the expedition leader said, you and Lopsong are the best two members of the team to carry the injured climber over the glacier, and on to the hospital. Going across the glacier will be your greatest challenge. Be careful."

Namka and Lopsong started off into the glacier as dark, scary clouds formed above. Soon it got much colder, and began to snow. The path was covered, but Namka and Lopsong kept going. They knew they must get the climber to the doctor without delay.

The wind blew hard, then harder. Thick heavy snowflakes filled the air so they could barely see. The air was so full of snowflakes, that they became lost. "If we stop moving, we will freeze to death," Namka shouted through the howling wind.

Lopsong stopped. He knew if they kept going, they would surely fall into a crevasse and be lost forever. Namka held onto Lopsong. They both knew... it may be the end.

iercing cold and frostbite crept into their hands and feet. Namka and Lopsong didn't know what to do. Suddenly, a hazy figure appeared in the swirling snow. What was it? Who was it? They squinted their eyes to see the mysterious figure in the storm. From out of the whiteness came the dark form of a large creature. "It's the Yeti!" cried Namka fearfully.

T hey felt small and paralyzed with fear as the Yeti came closer and closer. He stopped and towered over them. They stared into each other's eyes. All at once, Namka realized the Yeti wasn't going to harm them, and sensed the Yeti was there to help. Namka gathered the courage to speak, "There are many evil stories told about you, but I know now they just aren't true. You are a kind and gentle friend."

The Yeti nodded.

"How did he know we were here?" thought Namka. "I bet the Yeti knows everything about his mountain home of glaciers and mountains. He must have watched us climbing all along."

he Yeti led them across the glacier, carefully avoiding the deep gashes and cracks in the ice.

"Look, the lights of the hospital!" shouted Namka.

Namka and Lopsong were excited about their adventure with the Yeti. When they approached the small hospital, the door opened, and they were welcomed in. Everyone was amazed they had carried the injured climber through such a storm and across the dangerous glacier.

s Namka turned to introduce the one who had made it possible, the Yeti... had disappeared. Then suddenly off in the darkness, they heard a mysterious high-pitched whistle.

Namka and Lopsong looked at each other with a smile. Now they understood the special secret that was hidden in the mountains.

Special thanks to
the Sherpas of Nepal
and the Yeti.

Glossary

Abominable Snowman: A legendary large hairy humanoid that is reported to live in the highlands of the Himalayan mountains.

Avalanche: The swift and sudden fall of a mass of snow, ice or rocks down a mountain slope.

Crevasse: A deep opening or split in a glacier.

Glacier: A large body of ice and snow formed by falling snow and accumulating over the years. Glaciers move slowly down mountain slopes and valleys. They hold most of the world's supply of fresh water.

Khumbu: The name of an area in the highlands of Nepal, home of the Sherpas. The Khumbu is located just south of Mt. Everest. (sounds like " come-boo")

Mount Everest: The world's tallest mountain, (29,028 feet) located on the boundary of Nepal and Tibet in the Himalayas. Known to the Sherpas as Chomolungma, " Mother goddess of the world".

Namka: Sounds like, " Nom-ka"

Nepal: A small Kingdom located between India and Tibet in Asia.

Pheriche: A small village that is the located down the valley from Mt. Everest at an altitude of 14,000 feet. It's the home of tiny high altitude medical rescue clinic. (sounds like, " Fairy- chay")

Sherpa: A tribe of people that live in the high Himalayan mountain regions of Nepal. Namka is a Sherpa.

Yak: A large shaggy-haired wild ox that lives in the Tibetan and Nepalese highlands. Yaks can walk and climb at high altitudes for long distances with heavy loads. Lopsong is a yak.

Yeti: You know what a Yeti is. Did you find the Yeti tracks?

To order books or special presentation information contact:
The Spirit of Adventure, Ltd.
6022 So. Newport Street
Englewood, Colorado 80111-4435
Phone 303-779-4264 - Fax 303-220-9294

Library of Congress Cataloguing in Publication Data
Brian O'Malley
The Secret of the Mountains
Summary: A story of a sherpa boy and his yak and their adventures in
the mighty Himalaya mountains of Nepal.
Library of Congress Catalog Card number

92-61458
ISBN 0-9634446-0-3

This Book was Designed and Produced by
The Spirit of Adventure, Ltd. Denver, Colorado

Printed in Korea by Sung In Printing American, Inc.